Billy's Box

John Prater

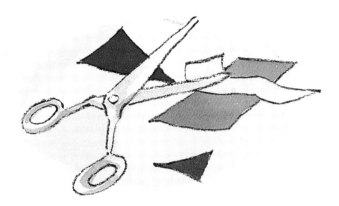

CAMBRIDGE
UNIVERSITY PRESS

Billy found a big box. He heard
a funny noise inside it.

It was a hedgehog!

"Hello!" said the hedgehog. "Look what I've got."

The hedgehog had some paper and some scissors. She said, "You can have the little scissors and I'll have the big scissors."

Billy cut out a little flower.

The hedgehog cut out a much bigger flower.
"Wow!" said Billy. "That's good."

Next, Billy cut out a row of trees.

The hedgehog cut out a great big forest
of trees.

"Wow!" said Billy. "That's good."

"Come and play in my forest," said
the hedgehog. She held Billy's hand and
led the way.

They went further and further into the
forest. The trees got bigger and bigger.

"Oh no!" said Billy. "I think we're lost.
I want to go home."

The hedgehog said, "Don't worry, Billy."
She began to cut down the trees with her big
scissors.

"That's better," said Billy. "But look at all this mess!"

"Watch me!" laughed the hedgehog. She rolled round the floor and all the paper stuck to her prickles.

Then it was time to say goodbye.

"Goodbye," said Billy.

"Goodbye, Billy," laughed the hedgehog.

Then Mum came in. "Shall we go for
a walk in the forest?" she said.